Juega, juega, juega, querido dragón

Play, Play, Play, Dear Dragon

por/by Margaret Hillert

ilustrado por/Illustrated by David Schimmell

NORWOOD HOUSE PRESS

Queridos padres y maestros:

La serie para lectores principiantes es una colección de lecturas cuidadosamente escritas, muchas de las cuales ustedes recordarán de su propia infancia. Cada libro comprende palabras de uso frecuente en español e inglés y, a través de la repetición, le ofrece al niño la oportunidad de practicarlas. Los detalles adicionales de las ilustraciones refuerzan la historia y le brindan la oportunidad de ayudar a su niño a desarrollar el lenguaje oral y la comprensión.

Primero, léale el cuento al niño; después deje que él lea las palabras con las que está familiarizado y pronto, podrá leer solito todo el cuento. En cada paso, elogie el esfuerzo del niño para que se sienta más confiado como lector independiente. Hable sobre las ilustraciones y anime al niño a relacionar el cuento con su propia vida.

Sobre todo, la parte más importante de la experiencia de la lectura es ¡divertirse y disfrutarla!

Shannon Cannon

Shannon Cannon
Consultora de lectoescritura

Dear Caregiver,

The *Beginning-to-Read* series is a carefully written collection of readers, many of which you may remember from your own childhood. This book, *Dear Dragon's Day with Father*, was written over 30 years after the first *Dear Dragon* books were published. The *New Dear Dragon* series features the same elements of the earlier books, such as text comprised of common sight words. These sight words provide your child with ample practice reading the words that appear most frequently in written text. The many additional details in the pictures enhance the story and offer the opportunity for you to help your child expand oral language skills and develop comprehension.

Begin by reading the story to your child, followed by letting him or her read familiar words and soon your child will be able to read the story independently. At each step of the way, be sure to praise your reader's efforts to build his or her confidence as an independent reader. Discuss the pictures and encourage your child to make connections between the story and his or her own life.

Above all, the most important part of the reading experience is to have fun and enjoy it!

Shannon Cannon

Shannon Cannon,
Literacy Consultant

Norwood House Press • P.O. Box 316598 • Chicago, Illinois 60631
For more information about Norwood House Press please visit our website at www.norwoodhousepress.com or call 866-565-2900.
Text copyright ©2010 by Margaret Hillert. Illustrations and cover design copyright ©2010 by Norwood House Press, Inc. All rights reserved. No part of this book may be reproduced or utilized in any form or by any means without written permission from the publisher.
Designer: The Design Lab

LIBRARY OF CONGRESS CATALOGING-IN-PUBLICATION DATA

Hillert, Margaret.
  [Play, play, play dear dragon. Spanish & English]
  Juega, juega, juega, querido dragon = Play, play, play dear dragon / por Margaret Hillert ;
illustrado por David Schimmell ; traducido por Eida Del Risco.
    p. cm. — (A beginning-to-read book)
  Summary: "A boy and his pet dragon spend a day at the playground and make a new friend"—Provided by publisher.
  ISBN-13: 978-1-59953-363-6 (library edition : alk. paper)
  ISBN-10: 1-59953-363-4 (library edition : alk. paper)
  [1. Dragons—Fiction. 2. Playgrounds—Fiction. 3. Spanish language materials—Bilingual.] I. Schimmell, David, ill. II. Del Risco, Eida. III. Title. IV. Title: Play, play, play dear dragon.
  PZ73.H55721 2010
  [E]—dc22

                                    2009041516

Manufactured in the United States of America in North Mankato, Minnesota. 161R-052010

Hay un lugar donde podemos jugar.

There is a spot where we can play.

Ya me levanté.
Tú también te debes levantar.
Quiero que vengas conmigo.

I am up now.
You have to get up, too.
I want you with me.

Vamos. Vamos.
Uno, dos, tres.
ARRIBA.

Come on. Come on.
One—two—three.
UPPPP—

Me voy a comer esto.
Me gusta.
Me hace bien.

I will eat this.
I like it.
It is good for me.

Come un poco.
Te hace bien.
Te hará crecer.

Have some of this.
It is good for you.
It will make you big.

Ahora vamos a buscar un lugar donde jugar.

Now we will find the spot where we can play.

Veo algo.
Lo veo.
Corre, corre, corre.

I see something.
I see it.
Run, run, run.

9

Váyanse. No pueden subir aquí.
No los quiero aquí.

Go away. You can not come up here.
I do not want you here.

Ay, no. Eso no estuvo bien.
Ahora no tengo amigos con quien jugar.
¿Qué puedo hacer?

Oh, no. That was not good.
Now I have no friends to play with.
What can I do?

Los voy a buscar.
Los voy a encontrar.

I will go look for them.
I will find them.

Lo siento. Quiero que seamos amigos.
Quiero jugar con ustedes.

I am sorry. I want to be friends.
I want to play with you.

Sí, sí. Podemos ser amigos.
Podemos ir a un buen lugar para jugar.

Yes, yes. We can be friends.
We can go to a good spot to play.

¡Mira! ¿Ves eso?

Oh, boy! Do you see that?

Podemos ir
ARRIBA, ARRIBA, ARRIBA.

We can go
UP, UP, UP.

Podemos ir ABAJO, ABAJO, ABAJO.

We can go DOWN,
DOWN,
DOWN.

Esto también es divertido.
Es divertido hacer esto.

This is fun, too.
It is fun to do this.

Ahora te ayudaré a hacer esto.

Now I will help you do this.

Y tú me puedes ayudar.
Me gusta hacer esto.

And you can help me.
I like to do this.

¿Puedes hacer esto? ¿Puedes hacerlo?
Uno y dos y tres...

Can you do this? Can you do it?
One, and two, and three—

Aquí está mi pelota.
Soy bueno en esto.
¿Quieres jugar conmigo?
Es divertido.

Here is my ball.
I am good at this.
Do you want to play with me?
This is fun.

Esto también es divertido.

This is fun, too.

Ahora tengo que irme. Mi mamá me llama.

I have to go now. My mother wants me.

Tú estás conmigo y yo estoy contigo.
Ha sido un buen día, querido dragón.

Here you are with me. And here I am with you.
What a good day, dear dragon.

READING REINFORCEMENT

The following activities support the findings of the National Reading Panel that determined the most effective components for reading instruction are: Phonemic Awareness, Phonics, Vocabulary, Fluency, and Text Comprehension.

Phonemic Awareness: The /ou/ sound

Sound Substitution: Say the words on the left to your child. Ask your child to repeat the word, changing the middle sound to the /**ou**/ sound.

moose = mouse	spat = spout	fund = found
grand = ground	catch = couch	shot = shout
pat = pout	load = loud	pond = pound
band = bound	horse= house	scoot = scout

Phonics: The letters o and u

1. Demonstrate how to form the letters **o** and **u** for your child.

2. Have your child practice writing **o** and **u** at least three times each.

3. Write down the following letters and spaces and ask your child to write the letters **o** and **u** on the spaces in each word:

gr_ _ nd	f_ _ nd	l_ _ d	c_ _ nt
s_ _ nd	_ _ t	m_ _ se	pr_ _ d
m_ _ th	fl_ _ r	r_ _ nd	h_ _ se

4. Ask your child to read each word.

Vocabulary: Making Words

1. Write the words "the playground" at the top of a piece of paper.

2. Write each letter in the words "the playground" on separate small pieces of paper.

3. Explain to your child that the letters in the words **the** and **playground** can be used to make new words.

4. Provide the following clues and help your child use the letters to make the correct words. Ask your child to write the words on the paper under "the playground".

- A word that describes what you can do for fun with your friends. (play)
- Where you plant seeds. (ground)
- What you do when you use money to buy something. (pay)
- A word used for weight. (pound)
- What you do when you get in bed. (lay)
- Something you use to carry things (like your food in the lunchroom). (tray)
- The color made by mixing white and black. (gray)
- Something you use to clean things. (rag)
- The part of your body that has hair, ears, and a face. (head)
- What you do when you look at the words and pictures in a book. (read)
- The shape of a circle. (round)

Fluency: Choral Reading

1. Reread the story with your child at least two more times while your child tracks the print by running a finger under the words as they are read. Ask your child to read the words he or she knows with you.

2. Reread the story aloud together. Be careful to read at a rate that your child can keep up with.

3. Repeat choral reading and allow your child to be the lead reader and ask him or her to change from a whisper to a loud voice while you follow along and change your voice.

Text Comprehension: Discussion Time

1. Ask your child to retell the sequence of events in the story.

2. To check comprehension, ask your child the following questions:
   - How do you think the boy felt on page 10 when the other boy told him he couldn't come up?
   - How did the problem get solved?
   - What is your favorite thing to do at the playground?
   - How do you make new friends?
   - What was your favorite part of the story? Why?

Margaret Hillert ha escrito más de 80 libros para niños que están aprendiando a leer. Sus libros han sido traducidos a muchos idiomas y han sido leídos por más de un millón de niños de todo el mundo. De niña, Margaret empezó escribiendo poesía y más adelante siguió escribiendo para niños y adultos. Durante 34 años, fue maestra de primer grado. Ya se retiró, y ahora vive en Michigan donde le gusta escribir, dar paseos matinales y cuidar a sus tres gatos.

Photograph by Glenna Washburn

ABOUT THE AUTHOR Margaret Hillert has written over 80 books for children who are just learning to read. Her books have been translated into many different languages and over a million children throughout the world have read her books. She first started writing poetry as a child and has continued to write for children and adults throughout her life. A first grade teacher for 34 years, Margaret is now retired from teaching and lives in Michigan where she likes to write, take walks in the morning, and care for her three cats.

ACERCA DEL ILUSTRADOR David Schimmell fue bombero durante 23 años, al cabo de los cuales guardó las botas y el casco y se dedicó a trabajar como ilustrador. David ha creado las ilustraciones para la nueva serie de Querido dragón, así como para muchos otros libros. David nació y se crió en Evansville, Indiana, donde aún vive con su esposa, dos hijos, un nieto y dos nietas.

ABOUT THE ILLUSTRATOR David Schimmell served as a professional firefighter for 23 years before hanging up his boots and helmet to devote himself to work as an illustrator. David has happily created the illustrations for the New Dear Dragon books as well as many other books throughout his career. Born and raised in Evansville, Indiana, he lives there today with his wife, two sons, a grandson and two granddaughters.